WEST OF IRELAND
Folk Tales for Children

Rab Fulton

Illustrated by Marina Wild

The History Press

For Jennie, Dylan and Callum

First published 2018

The History Press
The Mill, Brimscombe Port
Stroud, Gloucestershire, GL5 2QG
www.thehistorypress.co.uk

British Library Cataloguing in Publication Data.
A catalogue record for this book is available from the British Library.

ISBN 978 0 7509 8372 3

Typesetting and origination by The History Press
Printed and bound by CPI Group Ltd

Contents

1

The Curious Hill

Knockma is a curious hill. It rises up from the flat fertile plains of North Galway like the beer belly of a giant who drank too much a couple of eons ago and then lay down for a sleep and sank into the ground, leaving only his gigantic round gut sticking out. A gigantic gut that, over the centuries, became blanketed by soil and mulch and oak and ash and edible plants such as Herb Robert.

This is not entirely unlikely, as the west of Ireland was once absolutely stuffed full of mountain-sized people. But, like mountains, the giants all seem to have got a bit sleepy and they had pretty much vanished by the time Saint Patrick arrived on these shores. Imagining Knockma as a giant's belly is not a sign of foolishness; rather it is proof that you are blessed with a lively imagination and a good appreciation of the legends of the west. However, in actual fact Knockma is not a giant's belly. Rather, its shape is evidence of something far more magical.

If you take a walk up Knockma, you will encounter clues as to the true nature of the hill. Walkers follow a path that winds around the side of the hill facing the ruins of Castle Hacket. By unspoken agreement people normally follow the path in a clockwise direction. There may be nothing to this, just a simple case of people following the route of those in front of them, for even when it is quiet there are always other people on the hill.

But what is curious is the subtle atmosphere of the hill. Sometimes you may get a little tired – leg-weary, as it were – and think to yourself, 'I need some refreshment'. At that very instant a gentle flurry of rain will fall on you. Or perhaps the day has too much bleakness and dreichness about it, and your walk is suffering a little too much from the cold and dark. 'Oh, I wish it was warmer,' you mutter, and in that very instant the clouds part and strong sunlight wraps itself around you like a blanket or an embrace from the cosmos. It lasts only a moment but it perks you up and gives you the boost you need to continue walking.

The opposite may also happen. You begin your walk on a perfect day, warm with a little breeze. You are feeling in fine fettle, with your favourite walking boots on, a backpack filled with food and water, and good companions to share the journey with. Yet for all this positivity, the walk quickly becomes a drudge. Where there are trees overhead the air is thick and cloying. In the open, the wind is sharp or the sun too eager. Soon you and your friends feel energy and enthusiasm fading away. It is as if, on this particular day, the hill does not want visitors, and is making the point that it would prefer it if you left.

However, if you keep going the drained feeling will pass; soon enough your mood will lift and the walk will become a pleasure once more. If the hill was asking you to leave, it clearly does not want to make too big a deal of it. The hill is subtle and does not want to draw too much attention to the disturbing possibility that it may be able to think and be touched by moods and emotions.

The subtlety of atmospheric conditions on the hill and its surroundings have been commented on by many people. In the 1880s the antiquarian G.H. Kinahan noted that 'The soft breezes that pass one in an evening in West Galway are … said to be due to the flight of a band of the good people on their way to Cnockmaa (Hill of the Plain), near Castle Hackett, on the east of Lough Corrib … A soft hot blast indicates the presence of a good fairy; while a sudden shiver shows that a bad one is near.'

Knockma is clearly a hill with a reputation. It also has secrets that the path keeps visitors far away from. For the path only stays on the side of the hill facing the ruins of the ancient Castle Hacket Tower. It is a great path for walking, with woods and dips and bumps for exploring or wandering in. One of those dips is referred to as the fairy glen, but most people regard the name as a curiosity rather than a clue. However, what most people do not realise is that there are far more fascinating things to be seen up on the top of the hill, things that you could never guess at if you just followed the path.

If you do leave the path and scramble your way up the mulch-scented slope, past the short wind-sculpted and moss-clad trees, you will soon come to the very top of Knockma and see there the remains of huge prehistoric cairns, some of which may have been built nine thousand years ago. From the top you can look down on a landscape as clear and precise as any map. Look, there are the fertile farmlands that stretch up to Cong; and then from Cong we can follow Lough Corrib glittering its way south and south-east down towards Galway Bay; and beyond the Bay, softened by the vast distance, stand the hills of the Burren in County Clare. This one hill dominates it all.

The view and the great ancient stony mounds are the evidence that this hill has long been regarded as a unique and magical place. And this is rightly so, for Knockma is not merely a hill. It is in fact the palace of a very ancient and powerful being. His name is Finnbheara. He is a being with the power to make crops blossom or make crops wilt and fail. He has the military savvy to defeat the fairy armies that have been sent against him from the kingdoms of Munster, Leinster and Scotland, and yet the happy indifference of a child who laughs off such battles as mere games and momentary pleasures. He is the most powerful fairy in the two kingdoms of Ireland and Scotland, though his influence and power stretches well beyond this world into many others. For as well as being the king of the Connacht fairies, Finnbheara is the Lord of the Dead.

2

The Nature of Fairies

Before examining the history of Finnbheara and his kind, it is well to clarify a number of things. What is of particular importance is that the magical beings who exist alongside us do not approve of the word 'fairy'. It is a word that has become synonymous with pretty little creatures with gossamer wings and sparkly wands. These little creatures can be a bit naughty, like Tinkerbell in J.M. Barry's *Peter Pan*, but in the main they are as sweet as puppies. The creatures who live in Ireland

and Scotland are not sweet, and while they can appear pretty, they can also warp into horrific guises that would leave you trembling in fear for the remaining span of your life.

There are better ways of describing such beings. In Irish they are the *daoine sídhe*, 'the people of the mounds', as they live in hills. It is well also to refer to them politely as the *daoine maithe*, 'the good people', in the hope that they will look well on you, or perhaps at least not look ill upon you. Another way of encouraging the *daoine maithe* to look on you kindly is to leave little gifts as a mark of respect. These gifts can be as simple as a glass of wine or a cup of milk. In return the *daoine maithe* are content to allow us mere mortals to evoke their names in other rituals.

I have heard that in the poorer households of Scotland and Ireland there was once a meal-time tradition that involved children leaving a bit of food at the side of their plate for the 'wee man'. These little scraps of food were in fact what the mother of the household ate after her family had finished their meal. It

was a tradition that travelled the world with the hungry emigrants of these two nations. Five years or so ago I was talking to an elderly American woman who was visiting Galway to see the lands her ancestors had left. As we spoke she told me about her own childhood and in particular her Irish grandmother who told her to always remember to leave a little bit of food aside for the 'wee man'.

So the idea of 'fairies' can be used by humans for trickery, but if the trickery carries no ill will towards them, then the *daoine maithe* are happy enough to ignore it. Certainly there is no

account of the *daoine maithe* having ever being offended by the 'wee man' food ritual.

However, it is very important to remember that the *daoine maithe* are not always helpful. They are a capricious species. If it pleases them to do so, they will bring you good fortune. But, if their mood changes they can be wicked and cruel – their deeds may even be described as 'evil'. They kidnap the fairest-looking men, women and children. They have poisonous darts that they fire at farmhands and livestock. They ruin crops and rip off roofs.

What is the root of their anger, you may ask? Well, the trouble may be that these magical creatures are old, incredibly old, older even than the earth and the moon and the sun and the stars. Not only are they old, but they may even be immortal. Long after the moon fails and the seas gang dry, still these creatures will carry on existing in some form or other.

3

In the Beginning

Long before time began, long before this physical universe we inhabit came into being, there existed – and still exists – another realm, which for want of adequate words we mere mortals refer to as Heaven.

It is a place that defies description, for even those mortals who have glimpsed it in a vision are so overwhelmed by the experience that they find it impossible to recall any precise details. As Dante, the heartbroken poet, once explained, any impressions of Heaven dissolve as snow beneath the sun, or like prophecies writ on autumn leaves they are scattered and lost by the late-year winds. All that is left is a sense of incredible all-embracing sweetness.

Yet, as Heaven was the first home of the *daoine maithe*, some attempt must be made to give an impression of that realm. Dante asks us to imagine it as a rose vast beyond measure, with a labyrinth of paths weaving up and down and along its petals. Along these celestial tracks move the inhabitants of Heaven, angels with faces of living flame, wings of gold and robes of a whiteness so intense that 'no snow could match the whiteness they showed'.

Dante's Heaven also contains the souls of pious mortals, but we are interested in a far earlier age long before the existence of humans or planets, or even dust. A time when no universe existed, only a great and empty hollow.

Heaven, though, the immeasurable blossom, did exist far above the infinite void. Heaven was a place of perfect beauty, for between its great petals every object existed in its ideal form. The ideal table, the ideal horse, the ideal mountain, forest, river, the ideal sunset. Though whether it has the ideal example of absolutely everything

is less uncertain. What about the ideal knee scab, asks the curious child? Does such a thing exist to be peeled off and chewed and delighted in? What about the ideal rude joke about farts and bottoms?

The problem with trying to understand the early history of Heaven is that the information we have about it comes down to us from the accounts of long dead old men with big beards and even bigger bank accounts (or herds of goats, cattle, etc.) who got really annoyed if people asked them questions, particularly if the people asking the question were children or women or came from a different tribe. Of course this does not mean that the old men with big beards were mean or bad. Many of them strike me as quite pleasant and reasonably wise people, the sort of people you'd be quite happy to share a cuppa with or stroll along the beach at Salthill, though admittedly they might – like the Galway priests of recent memory – start twitching when they see women and men swimming in the sea together.

The point I'm trying to make is that while it's always good to respect our hirsute elders, it's perhaps not always a good idea to completely trust their take on things. So, yes, Heaven was, is and always shall be a very beautiful place, but it did have, has and always will have its own little problems. Not the least of these is that while an ideal sunset is a hashtag awesome thing to experience, there may be other ideal things that are not so good. For example, the ideal mistake, the ideal argument, the ideal bout of senseless violence. All of these have occurred in Heaven, though we prefer to ignore them in the way we pretend to ignore the fact that little Aoife is chewing her scabs at the dinner table, while Ruaridh's finger is thrust deeply up his nose.

But I am wandering off a little. All we need to know is that long before humans existed, Heaven was filled with a perfectly beautiful race of beings which we know as angels. All were perfect in form, their skin unblemished by wrinkle or scar, their silken robes resistant to all dirt or stains. As they walked they shone; as they shone they added to the lustre of their realm. Among the ranks of these majestic beings who walked the maze of paths or flew around the great petals like industrious yet happy bees were Finnbheara and his wife Oonagh, as content with life as all the other divine beings.

There was no compulsion on the angels to do anything, though many did find a role for themselves. Gabriel, to pick one example, delighted in transmitting messages across the infinite flower (we can think of him perhaps as the Postmaster General). Meanwhile other angelic beings such as Venus, Tu Er Shen and Hathor were experts in event management, organising parties filled with music, dance and love. Occasionally these parties could, as parties do, get a little too rowdy, with arguments and even fisticuffs. Fortunately, there were many skilled in healing any physical or emotional hurt; one of the most talented being Brigid, a friend of Oonagh and Finnbheara.

In addition to these, there was a band of grim yet handsome angels clad in chainmail and leather, who made sure all was orderly and well in the great blossom and that conflicts were resolved amicably. The leader of these – the Garda Commissioner of Heaven, as it were – was a creature who was as inflexible as he was incorruptible. His name was Lucifer and he was the constant companion of the greatest of all the sacred beings. She was known simply as God and it was her sacred light that gave life to the heavenly rose and all its inhabitants.

Heaven was perfection. But I mentioned earlier that such perfection was not always to the good. For in time, the ideal mistake would be made, the ideal argument would result, and the ideal bout of senseless violence would erupt. How Finnbheara, Oonagh and their companions responded to this would have repercussions that would shape the history and culture of a small country that did not then exist. A country we now know as Ireland.

4

God's New Policy

Gabriel ran an efficient service for transmitting God's messages – usually these were minor updates on existing regulations. However, one day Gabriel brought a message that was very different. It called on all angels to attend a meeting where God would announce a new policy. This caused some gossip but no great sense of concern among the heavenly ranks. Certainly there is no record of any of the divine beings feeling worried or even afraid. Whether God herself anticipated the terrible fallout from her policy talk is something that theologians have been arguing about for a long, long time.

On the day of the announcement God stood on a small hill, dressed in glowing raiment. She nodded and smiled politely as arriving angels greeted her. To her side stood Lucifer, his chainmail glittering and his eyes watching the gathering crowd. When all the angels had gathered, God spoke.

'All of you have the free will to make decisions for good and for ill. However, you have never felt the need to exercise this. Thanks to my bright love, you all live in a perfect and incorruptible place. Thanks to the diligence of Lucifer, any minor mistakes and problems have been resolved before they can escalate. Choice and responsibility are something you are capable of, but up to now have had no reason to think about. And because of this, I fear you may be stunted in your cognitive development.'

'Speak for yourself,' quipped one of the angels.

'What's a cog-nog-ititiv development?' whispered another.

'Shh,' muttered another, 'let her finish.'

'I have decided, therefore,' continued God in a quiet yet firm voice, 'that there will be new beings brought into existence.'

Before her the angels became more animated, some looking around to gauge the response of friends, others whispering opinions. One called out, 'We don't need new angels. There's no room for them.'

Lucifer stepped forward and looked at the crowd. The angels fell silent. Lucifer returned to God's side.

'These new beings will not be angels, they will be humans. Their bodies will age and sicken and finally fail them. Because of this you immortal beings will be far superior to them.'

'That's all right, then. You had us worried for a while there.' The mood in the crowd lightened.

God glanced at Lucifer, who once more stepped forward and gazed at the crowd. When there was silence he returned to God's side. Most of the assembled angels were filled with curiosity and anticipation, but some were getting bored. Oonagh nudged Finnbheara, who was beginning to yawn.

God spoke once more: 'It will be your role to oversee these mortals and to give what aid and guidance you can, as long as it does not interfere with their free will.'

Finnbheara swallowed his yawn, rubbed his hands with glee and nudged his wife. 'That sounds more like it. We can have mighty fun with these new fellows.'

The guardian of Heaven remained by God's side but felt uneasy as he listened to snatches of the nearest conversations. While many angels were delighted at the promise of these new beings, others remained unconvinced that mortals were to be welcomed.

'If they have free will, that makes them the same as us, no matter how long they live.'

'They will take God's love away from us.'

'Oh, it is worse than that. Think on it. The lives of these new human beings will be miniscule compared to ours. Would that not mean that everything they feel in their short lives will have greater intensity than anything we experience? Their sorrows will be sharper. Their joys greater and fuller. Their passions, arts and thoughts will have an importance vaster than ours. Even human follies and mistakes will have greater worth than angelic achievements.'

Some angels shouted the speaker down. But others demanded he be allowed to speak. Lucifer braced himself, but God laid her hand gently on his. 'Let them talk,' she said.

Lucifer's unease deepened when, looking towards his beautiful companion, he saw that her face was wet with tears and her voice quivered as she quietly said, 'Give them a few minutes more, my love, then call them to order again, for I have one more announcement to make.'

Beautiful gowns were torn as confused and angry angels grabbed at each other and demanded their opinion be heard. When Lucifer could stand it no more he clapped his hands together and the sound echoed around Heaven. The angels stopped their arguing in an instant. They looked to the hill, their expressions sheepish and contrite. Some shook their heads as if they had just awoken from some strange unsettling dream of anger and menace.

God wiped her eyes and stepped forward. 'I have one more announcement. Until now we have all existed in perfect harmony. Instinctively we each knew our place and our role, and there has been no need for formal titles and positions. But the creation of these new beings may bring confusion into our ranks. Therefore I say it is necessary that we clarify where each of us stands. As it is my light that gives all life, I ask that you recognise that I rank above you in the same way as you rank above the mortal humans. I rule and I rule alone. Only by recognising this will we ensure that there is order and peace.'

'Hurrah for God!' cheered many of the angels. But some wailed, 'We are reduced, shrunken.' Others, filled with anger, rushed at God shouting and gesturing. Frightened that she would be hurt, one angel by the name of Michael pushed his way to God's side and called for aid from Lucifer. But Lucifer understood that God's words meant that he would no longer be her constant companion, that he would simply be one more angel, far beneath God's lonesome status. So sudden and abrupt was the weight of grief and betrayal on his heart that his legs almost buckled under him, even as angry and scared voices swirled around him in a dizzying tumult.

Who threw the first spear is not recorded, but in a moment the beautiful rose of Heaven was infested with the clamour and din of war. Michael called on the angels to defend God. Lucifer, transforming into a great dragon, demanded the angels support him as the chief guardian of Heaven's constitution. The fighting was as savage as it was long. Harmony was smashed by chaos. Where once there had been song, now there were screams and groans. Where once there had been gentle parties and meetings of old friends, now there was the clash and clang of vast legions of warriors. Not one inch of Heaven was untouched by war. Even on the very edge of Heaven, those angels who fled the war were assailed by the distant echo of monstrous weaponry, booming like the sound of pebbles rolled and tossed by an ever-moving and ever-grinding tide. It is among these refugees we find those magical beings that would eventually be known as the *daoine maithe*.

Why did some angels refuse to take sides? Perhaps out of fear. Perhaps in shock at how swiftly the war erupted. Maybe there were those who only wanted to have time to consider

the opposing arguments before taking sides.
There may even have been those who were
waiting for the armies of God and Lucifer
to become so exhausted that they could then
step in and take over Heaven. Many, I guess,

were simply appalled at the savagery. Wishing only for things to be as they once were, many desperately prayed that the war would finish as quickly as it began.

But there was no swift end to the battling. The violence became so great that it spilled out of Heaven and into the great emptiness below. The emptiness shook and echoed with scorching heat and blasts of terrifying anger. Then the great dragon tail of Lucifer broke through the fabric of Heaven and ignited our universe into existence.

Stars were birthed from nuclear and chemical reactions; burning masses of rock collided with bomb-blast-fast icy shrapnel; huge gravitational wells pulled and pummelled matter into the shapes of asteroids and planets. As God's battalions slowly ground down the ranks of Lucifer's followers, so too did our universe begin to settle into order and harmony.

5

Punishment and Exile

There is no sadder sight than a rose wilted by frost, its once bright petals blackened from the blight of insects. We can only imagine how God wept as she looked at the rose of Heaven broken and ugly after eons of war. In time she and the angels would replenish the divine blossom until it shone more brightly than ever. But in the immediate aftermath of conflict God had a more pressing concern.

After deep consideration God decided Lucifer and his followers were to be cast out

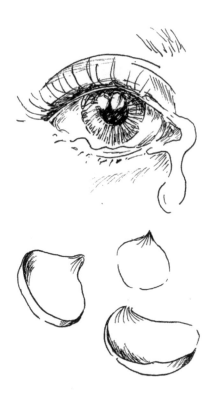

of Heaven. Lucifer became known by many other names including Satan, the Devil and the Earl of Hell. His followers became known as demons. The epitome of all things foul, wicked and ruinous, they were sentenced to an eternity imprisoned in fire. Where these flames are, it is hard to say. Perhaps they are in another universe, a universe constructed entirely from blaze. Or perhaps each of the insurgent angels were cast into the belly of one of the innumerable stars of our universe, to be whipped by the ferocity of nuclear explosions. Perhaps the great jets of plasma that occasionally erupt out from the star we circle are caused by one such demon flailing in frustration.

Though Lucifer was defeated and cast from Heaven into fire, he was not reduced by this. He remains a constant threat with the potential to defeat God. But his threat is in the manner of the wind that blows and beats against the vanes of a wind turbine, its potential to destroy being converted into energy instead. So too the constant tension between Lucifer and God creates the dynamic that gives power to reality. For this reason it is important to respect Lucifer, even as we fear him.

But I digress, for Lucifer and his followers were not the only angels that troubled God. She also had to figure out what to do about those angels who, rather than taking sides, had fled the trauma of war. They had not betrayed God, but they had not helped. After some thought God decided they were to be sent into exile. There they would remain until judgement day, when God would declare her final decision.

And so these exiles fell from Heaven's grace and tumbled through the great void of the cosmos. Though powerful beings in their own right, against the vastness of space they were as insignificant as motes of dust. Perhaps it was during this great falling that we find the origin of the music of the fairies. For the galaxies they tumbled through served as sounding boards that echoed with the crackle of asteroids spinning, the pulsing boom and hiss of storm-wracked gas giants, and the distant radiating roar and spit of suns dying and birthing. With every such alien noise assailing and drenching them, the angels knew they were falling ever further from the joy and harmony of Heaven's melody.

So it was that, eons later, when the exiled angels tried to make music that reflected the beauty of their lost home, the sounds they produced, though full of beauty and grace, were also touched with vast sorrow and foreboding; beneath every glittering beat that danced and skipped there waited a deep dark cosmic discord. It is this conflict that gives the music of the immortals such power and resonance, yet makes it so dangerous for humans to hear. As Lady Wilde warned us more than a century ago, the sorrow and the ecstasy of the fairy music can easily transport us mere mortals into a state of 'forgetfulness of all things, and sometimes into the sleep of death'.

As the angels fell, the place of their exile took shape. Even though the war between God and Lucifer had finished, the material world still roiled and shook in the wake of the titanic conflict. In the far corner of the universe the outer wisps of a vast nebula collapsed under the impact of an exploding star, creating a great disc of fiery material. The pressure was so great that hydrogen fused with helium, creating an astounding burst of energy and, just as a phoenix is born from fire, so our star was born. Like every newborn creature, our sun was ravenous and ate up nearly all the material spinning around it. Yet there were crumbs enough left over to form the planets of our solar system.

6

Life on Earth

Earth spent much time as a ball of burning lava, but gradually it cooled enough for rain to fall and oceans and lakes to form. The atmosphere was still poisonous, but the chemicals needed for life could be found sloshing around in a reeking witch's brew that held the potential for every and any form of life, from eye of newt and toe of frog, wool of bat and tongue of dog. It may well have been supercharged lightning that set off the chemical reactions that kick-started evolution, but accompanying the flash there would also have been a sound. And the sound, I have no doubt, would have been the cackle of an old woman, the Cailleach, the creator being of Scottish and Irish folklore.

Though her story is not included in this book (it would take volumes to write a biography of such an important and controversial character), a little has to be said about the Cailleach, not least because she helped shape and continues to shape this world. Earth is a restless planet; nothing is ever settled or finished, its mountains feeling as compelled as clouds to change shape (though more slowly). But in addition to the likes of meteorology, volcanism, plate tectonics and evolution there were and are other less understood forces. The Cailleach is one of the most potent and dangerous of these.

In her original form she was a giantess who strode across Scotland and Ireland with a hammer in her hand and a basket filled with monstrous rocks (harvested, some say, from Scandinavia). She hammered mountains into shape, tore at coastlines, scattered her massive rock boulders along shorelines, and gouged holes in the land that filled with water and so became rivers and loughs. Hers was and is a power that demands respect. Even after the landscapes of Ireland and Scotland pleased her eye, she was not content. She continues as the weaver of storms, the creator of bleakest winter and the mistress of death. Behind all things that bring terror there stands the Cailleach. Her name translates into English as Old Woman, Hag or Witch – three designations that evoke strong negative reactions.

Once upon a time, however, the Old Woman, Hag and Witch – the myriad Cailleach – were viewed with awe and profound respect. A shift in perspective can make us understand why this would be. Yes, the sharp-edged, chasm-gouged mountain can be a terrible place, filled with treacherous footpaths, avalanches and fearful drops. Yet it is also the mountains that store the snow and ice of winter to release it in springtime as melt-waters that quench the thirst of the lowlands. Winter, though often cruel, also brings great blessings, for it is winter that compels plants to transfer energy downwards, making their roots go deeper into the soil, thus strengthening the foundations of

oak and ash and hazel tree. As for death, it is the completion of life, and its presence compels us mortals to live as fully and satisfyingly as we can, to dig and taste deeper the rich soil of experience, friendship, love, work, play, joy, grief, birth and marvellous adventures.

In some aspects the Cailleach shares much with benevolent God; in other ways she has all the terrifying rage of embittered Lucifer. It is impossible to say which she is closer to – it may be that she is in fact older than either. All that can be said with certainty is that without the Cailleach ours would be a shallower, less worthy existence.

7

The Testimony of Fintan Mac Bochra

And so the angels of this narrative tumbled from Heaven, and after immeasurable time came to rest in lands given shape by the Cailleach. Much has already been written about this early phase of their exile on earth and as my focus is on their later adventures I do not want to spend too much time on this period. However, this early history does hold important clues as to the character of the creatures we now commonly refer to as fairies.

Medieval scholars examined the history of the fallen angels in much detail, referring to them as the *Tuatha Dé Danann*. *Tuatha* was a medieval Irish term commonly understood to mean a tribe or small kingdom. In this context, however, a better description would be 'community of the mother goddess Danu'. It is uncertain where exactly the exiles landed; somewhere in northern Europe is the best guess. Next to nothing is known of this period, but it is interesting to note that by the time they arrived in Ireland, the exiles, who had fled the battlegrounds of Heaven, had mastered the art of warfare.

They arrived in the west of Ireland surrounded by a thick mist and, burning their ships so that they could not retreat, advanced against the then rulers of Ireland, the Firbolg. The war that ensued was as savage as it was short, with all the brave deeds and slaughter of the ten-year Trojan War compressed into less than a week. The battles roared and screamed across a vast landscape, a scarlet-splashed tide of ferocity that ebbed and flowed from the shores of Lough Mask to the foothills of Knockma.

The Firbolg finally retreated from battle, but the peace that followed was uneasy, with the victors having to cope with continued Firbolg threats. More dangerous was an armed revolt by the Fomorians, a race of giants allied to, or perhaps subservient to, the Firbolg. The Fomorians in turn were defeated, but were treated with respect by their new masters and allowed to live in peace in Connacht. The *Tuatha Dé Danann* had clearly mastered diplomacy as well as warfare.

Having defeated the Firbolg, the new overlords of Ireland began to settle the land. It may have been during this period that Finnbheara and Oonagh took up residence in Knockma, but how that came about is anybody's guess.

They are a clever pair, and I can imagine them using trickery to gain the hill. Perhaps the other *Tuatha Dé Danann* argued over who should own the hill, and Oonagh and Finnbheara offered to be temporary stewards:

> **Oonagh**: 'As soon as things are resolved among yourselves we'll give the hill back, gladly.'
> **Finnbheara**: 'Gladly and with great relief. We don't want to look after it, but duty is duty.'
> **Oonagh**: 'It'll be an onerous task, all that dusting and cleaning.'
> **Finnbheara**: 'But we know our duty. We'll keep it ship-shape and clean as a whistle.'
> **Oonagh**: 'And when your little contretemps is amicably concluded, we'll leave the hill quicker than quick.'
> **Finnbheara**: 'Swifter than a sneeze, we'll blow out of there. Cross our fingers, hope to die, duty is duty and all that stuff.'

Then, once they got the keys, as it were, they shut the bolt, blew a raspberry or two at their fuming compadres and settled into their fabulous new abode.

Or maybe they simply won it over a game of chess.

Your guess is as good as mine.

What is not in dispute, however, is that before Finnbheara and Oonagh moved in the *Tuatha Dé Danann* explored the curious hill all over. On the very crest they discovered a peculiar structure. It was a small artificial hill made up of tens of thousands of shards of grey stone.

Among the defeated Firbolg was a creature who claimed to know what the structure was. This creature was similar in appearance to the *Tuatha Dé Danann*, only smaller and twisted by old age. It was one of the mortal beings that God had spoken of, and the foretelling of which had caused violence to erupt in Heaven. The human was named Fintan Mac Bochra and he explained the stony mound thus:

'This is the burial site of Ceasair, the granddaughter of Noah. She argued with the patriarch and fled with her companions. The company included fifty women and three men. I, Fintan, was one of those men. We built our own small fleet of arks and escaped the flood that way. As we made our journey I fell in love with Ceasair, but she was our leader, and she would have no favourites.

'We reached the south of this island and tried to settle there. It is a good land, but there were not enough of us. We battled wolves and weather both, argued among ourselves and made foolish mistakes. Constantly we were moving on, seeking a place that all agreed would provide security and plenty. It took us many years but eventually we came to the fastness of Knockma. It was a perfect place to live, yet by the time we arrived there age and disease had brought an end to many a one's journey through this life.

'On Knockma we few survivors settled. By then time had thinned my hair and weakened my bones, but I hoped that my love would finally be repaid. It was not to be. In anger and sorrow I left the company of Ceasair and her remaining companions. I began what I believed would be my last journey. I grew ever older and slower as I wandered far across this land. My anger and sorrow grew old and slow too. Yet my love for Ceasair returned as young and quick as ever it had been. So I chose to return to Knockma, to die in the company of Ceasair.

'But I returned too late. Ceasair – the strongest, the bravest and most determined of us – was dead. She had outlived all her companions except me. With the last of my strength I placed her body on top of the hill. It rained hard and I trembled with cold and grief but I managed to use the last of my strength to build a cairn over her. Then I lay down and awaited death.

'But Knockma is not only the most visible of hills, it is the most ancient and magical. Instead of death I experienced transformation. I became a salmon and slipped down the rain-drenched sides of the hill. I slipped and tumbled until I came to a river. There I swam, the waters washing away old age. Then I became a bird and soared above my sorrows. Finally I became a mortal man again.

'I aged, but slowly, so slowly. Where other mortals live no longer than three score years and ten, I lived for millennia. I have seen much and experienced more, but my unique longevity brought terrible loneliness. When the Firbolg arrived in Ireland they shared their company with me, and I shared my knowledge with them. They became my new companions, though I have never forgotten Ceasair and tend her cairn whenever I can.'

From the testimony of Fintan Mac Bochra the *Tuatha Dé Danann* learned two things: that Knockma held a deep reserve of magic that could be added to their own considerable powers, and that most humans live no longer than seventy years and need not be feared or even thought about.

What Heaven's exiles failed to learn from the ancient's account was that humans, though mortal and often foolish, are capable of great courage and determination. This flaw in the knowledge of the immortals would be their undoing.

8

Of Gods and Men

The new home of the *Tuatha Dé Danann* was a place of great beauty. Dark cool forests, flower-and-fowl tapestried meadows, chortling rivers and shorelines where waves snatched at sun darts or tossed and foamed in the wind. It was a land that at times appeared almost as rich and beautiful as Heaven itself. Yet wiser heads among the *Tuatha Dé Danann* should have recalled how fragile Heaven was and how swiftly it was lost to them.

Many years passed. It may have been decades, or it may have been centuries or millennia: it is hard to measure time when talking of immortals. But years did pass, and there were many of them. The *Tuatha Dé Danann* felt secure and unthreatened. They feasted, made music, fell in and out of love, as carefree and innocent as children in a playground, messing and frolicking and inventing all manner of games and stories.

But even the best of girls and boys can display moments of selfishness and petty cruelty. It is all part of learning and growing, and most children – though sadly not all – come to understand that kindness is a far more effective tool for making friends and earning respect. But the *Tuatha Dé Danann* lacked the wisdom of children. Their lives were perfect, so what need was there to make new friends or earn respect from others? What need even to share any of the bounty of the island with each other?

And so they quarrelled among themselves.

It was during such a petty squabble between two or three of the immortal lords that something quite unexpected happened. They were squabbling over which precise piece of woodland, river, shoreline and stretch of golden sand belonged to which one of the lords, when a new voice spoke up: 'This is a silly discussion. This land is so big, there is bounty enough for everyone.'

The lords turned to see who had dared interrupt them. To their amazement they saw that the speaker was a mortal man. He was small, dark and smiling. He was Ith, a poet from the land of the Milesians. But the immortals were not interested in making introductions. Instead, angered that such a minor creature should dare interrupt them, they clenched their powerful fists and fell upon the mortal wordsmith.

They beat Ith until they thought he was dead, then, laughing, they left him, their silly argument now forgotten. But Ith was not dead. Badly wounded, he made his way back to the coast. There waited his companions, a small band of adventurers who had travelled to this far-off green island to see what they could discover. Having discovered violence, they quickly fled in their small boat, taking dying Ith with them.

They returned many months later, but this time they were accompanied by a huge armada. Outraged at the killing of a beloved poet, the Milesians vowed to punish the rulers of the green island.

Seeing the fleet of ships on the horizon, the *Tuatha Dé Danann* were unconcerned. They had no doubt that their great magical powers would crush those who threatened the land they ruled and loved. There was no need to apologise or make reparation for the killing of Ith. The mortal women and men who stared out from the boats would be destroyed easily and utterly.

But human courage is greater than any magic. Though they died in their thousands, the mortal warriors refused to be defeated. On they came with swords, spears and axes glinting until, shocked and stupefied by the

onslaught, the *Tuatha Dé Danann* cried out
'We surrender!'

The terms of peace that the Milesians offered
seemed generous. Each group would take
control of one half of the land. Only after the

Tuatha Dé Danann agreed did they learn the true meaning of the treaty. The half belonging to the mortal humans was the land above the ground, while the immortal *Tuatha Dé Danann* were consigned to the lands below.

Over time the relationship between humans and immortals has evolved and changed, but this first bargain has held firm. To this day we, the descendants of the Milesians, control those places that are touched by the light of the sun, moon and stars. The *Tuatha Dé Danann* remain in the places of shadow, most notably the hollow places beneath hills and mounds. And so they became the people of the mounds, *daoine sídhe*, though respectful (and fearful) mortals also refer to them as the *daoine maithe,* the good people.

The *daoine maithe* never lost their love for Ireland. If anything their love became more intense, resulting in occasional angry fits of jealousy and malice towards humans. More positively, this love motivated the fallen angels to reach a deeper understanding and appreciation of every aspect of this island. As

shape-shifters they often travelled abroad in a
wide variety of forms: beetles, birds, rodents,
fish, foxes and sea serpents; sometimes they

even journeyed as gusts of wind. In time their understanding of the rhythm and dynamism of nature came to match that of the ancient Cailleach.

Theirs was and is a great and generous *grá* for this land. Not only did individual members of the fallen angels specialise in studying different aspects of nature; they were willing to share their hard-won knowledge. The new rulers of Ireland gladly used the expertise of the defeated immortals. Soon they began to pay homage to their immortal teachers. Indeed, for a brief moment Heaven's exiles were so revered that they were worshipped as gods. Gods of wind. Gods of wheat. Gods of the shoreline. Gods of healing herbs. Gods of death and gods of love.

But this harmony did not last long.

9

End Days

The problem was that there was an empire called the Roman Empire and it fell. I'm not sure how it fell. My guess is that it was not paying enough attention to where it was going – maybe it was a bit too giddy or maybe it was having a tantrum – and so it did not see the brick, scooter, banana skin, football, or whatever it was in front of it, tripped over the object and fell.

It was a bad fall. So bad that a lot of people who lived in the Roman Empire thought that the end of the world had arrived. One of those people who feared this was a man called Patrick.

Though a Roman Christian, Patrick had lived much of his formative years in pagan Ireland where he had been taken as a slave. Patrick loved Ireland. He wanted to give the Irish the gift of the Christian faith. Now that the world was ending and judgement day was at hand it was really, really important that he return to Ireland. Time was running out; if his beloved Irish did not embrace Christianity then they would be cast into Hell.

Now, Hell as we know it was invented by a Greek thinker called Plato, who lived about eight hundred or so years before Saint Patrick. A lot of people, when they think of Plato, imagine him as an old bearded guy wearing a dusty robe who spent far too long writing long, boring, barely understandable tracts about really boring things. In my opinion, though, Plato was a wonderful writer: his words bubble and spark with humour, inventiveness and incredible descriptive power. Admittedly, some of his ideas were a wee bit wacky, but wacky in a completely mind-blowing way. Hell is definitely one of his wackier ideas.

Hell, as proposed by Plato, was the ideal form of punishment, torture and pain for people who undermined proper authority in this world. It was a punishment that you could never escape as it happened after death. Everybody dies, so everybody can be threatened with Hell. Plato reckoned a belief in Hell could be a good thing as it would stop people arguing with their betters or creating the kind of social and political upheaval that led to the death of Plato's beloved friend Socrates.

By the time the Roman Empire fell Plato's Hell had evolved into a horrifying punishment that only good Christians could hope to avoid. Non-Christians had no chance of escaping the big fire. Patrick suffered great mental pain as he truly believed that the Irish were all going to be sent to Hell unless he converted them, and converted them fast. Thus the conversion of the Irish began with a desperately terrified and terrifying love.

All other gods and faiths were false, declared Patrick and his followers. Their shrines were to be broken, their worshippers defeated

and humiliated. Even nature was a threat to the creed of the One God. According to this ideology forests, hills, rivers, the very shorelines and rocks – all were potential hiding places for evil beings that could snatch or tempt the Irish down to Hell. In this new world there was to be no more co-operation with Heaven's fallen angels.

And yet even the new masters of Ireland could not help but be mesmerised by the magical stories that surrounded them. So moved were the monks that they wrote down the stories for future generations to wonder at. It is said that this process began when Patrick ordered his scribes to write down the words of the dying Fianna warrior Oisín, who had returned to Ireland after living centuries on the magical isle of Tír na nÓg. Yet, in the writing the stories changed, much in the way that Ireland changed during Oisín's absence – the mortal and immortal heroes became reduced to mere characters in tales of wonder to amuse and delight.

Condemned as demons or fairytale curiosities, the *daoine maithe* retreated once more into the shadows, hollows and hills of Ireland and Scotland.

Of all the hills, Knockma remains the most prestigious. Inside it Lord Finnbheara and

Lady Oonagh remain, awaiting judgement day and hopefully the end of their exile from Heaven. They and their entourage enjoy life in their hidden realm. They feast and frolic, play music and dance, and make war against any other fairy bands that try to usurp them. Their love of Ireland and nature is as acute as ever, and they often journey above ground in the guise of creatures.

Over millennia they gained much wisdom about our world and considerable knowledge of the realms beyond this. Understandably they have mixed feelings about the mortals who walk freely in the daylight. They will play cruel jests on us or even kidnap the more beautiful among us. However, the following stories will show that despite their jealousy and bitterness, the immortals are still willing to share their knowledge and insights with those who treat Ireland, nature and the 'good people' with respect.

10

Lord Kirwan's Bride

Once upon a time there was a young lord who was looking for a wife. His name was Lord Kirwan and his family owned the green and fertile land surrounding Knockma. Or, more accurately, his family owned the land above the ground that surrounds Knockma. For, as everybody knows, the territory beneath the ground, the hidden hollows, grottoes and tunnels that stretch over countless miles and dimensions belong to Lord Finnbheara and Lady Oonagh.

The Kirwans had owned land in this area for hundreds of years, but in the late eighteenth century their wealth and influence increased massively. Like many of the leading Galway families whose emblems flutter in Eyre Square to this day, the Kirwans' wealth was partly a product of slave labour in the Caribbean. Men, women and children 'stolen from Africa', as the bard says, toiled ceaselessly and endured great cruelty to ensure that the finest families of Galway could have money enough to buy estates, horses and political power.

With this new wealth Lord Kirwan's grandfather expanded his estate around Knockma and built a fine new home, Castle Hackett House (the family's previous occasional residence was a rundown Anglo-Norman building, Castle Hackett Tower). Having moved into the fine mansion old Kirwan made sure to pay due respect to the immortal lord and lady who lived inside the nearby hill. Once a year he left a large barrel of finest wine outside the kitchen door, a barrel that would magically vanish overnight.

The next Lord Kirwan had a closer relationship with Finnbheara, so much so that when the lord found himself in debt, the king of the Connacht fairies rode his horse for him in a race, and won him a fortune.

The Lord Kirwan of this story, the son of the horse-race gambler, was not as respectful towards the king and queen of the 'good people'. Perhaps, being more assured of his power and wealth, he felt less need to treat his immortal neighbours with proper courtesy. Yet there were plenty of recent accounts of what the immortals were capable of.

Just before his grandfather had settled in Castel Hackett House, the alarm was raised in Connacht that an army of Scottish immortals was set to invade the west of Ireland. The invaders took on the shapes of beetles and, having made landfall, set out to destroy every tree, flower and cereal crop in their path. But a fairy host, also in the guise of beetles, led by Finnbheara and Oonagh, poured out from their fastness of Knockma and routed the Scottish invaders. Not for the first time had the military prowess of the Knockma immortals saved Connacht from ruin.

A more troubling occurrence took place not long after old Lord Kirwan had settled into the new family mansion. He and one of his sons were out riding when they were met by Lady Oonagh, dressed in her finest robes and riding on a great black horse. She took one look at the young lad and demanded he be given into her care. 'He will live in my palace beneath Knockma. He will dance every night and never grow old.' But old Lord Kirwan refused to hand his son over. 'So be it,' shrugged Lady Oonagh. That very night the boy fell ill. The finest physicians that money could buy were sent for, but to no avail. The boy grew sicker and died within three days. It seemed that a yearly casket of wine was not payment enough for the nobles beneath the hill.

Yet, even though the boy who had died was his own uncle, the new Lord Kirwan took little heed of such recent history. If asked about the fallen angels next door, he would dismiss them with a flick of his hand. 'Sure, they can drink

wine and ride horses,' he would say. 'Any mortal can do the same.' This then was the man who sent agents around Galway and Mayo to find a suitable wife to live with him in Castle Hackett House.

It took a while, for there were many women who would be Lord Kirwan's spouse. Spoilt for choice, the young lord often joked, 'I would marry them all if I could.' He no sooner set his mind on one women than his eye would go roving over another. But his advisors insisted a marriage must be made, and made soon. A wife not only brought children, but provided an entirely free household management service. She would look after house and servants, freeing up more of Lord Kirwan's time for work and pleasure. The lord sat down and consulted his notes. There was one woman who stood out from the rest, and if he must marry, then she would make the perfect bride.

The woman in question had clever eyes and a wry smile. Her fingers were nimble at sewing and even nimbler at catching false notations in an account ledger. She met with Lord Kirwan, found him suitable for her own ambitions, and agreed that he might call on her, which he did. Theirs was a match based on sound business and financial sense, but the more they met the closer they grew, for love is a hardy rose that, given the opportunity, will bloom in poor soil as well as rich.

So the pair were wed. It was a fine wedding and the festivities were even finer. The wedding guests were invited to Castle Hackett House for feasting, drinking, music, song and dancing. The house filled with the scent of candles, warm wine and perfumes, and echoed with the gay tinkle of the newest music and the newest gossip. Arm in arm the Lord and Lady Kirwan moved among the guests – landowners, merchants, bankers, politicians and religious leaders – greeting them all and making sure they were merry. However, not all the great and powerful had been invited to celebrate the marriage. No invitation had been sent to the immortal lord and lady who lived under the hill.

During the festivities, some of the guests observed a large beetle scuttling about. One moment it was spied on the floor, deftly avoiding dancing feet; then it was seen briefly on a table considering the rich foods there. It was shooed from the table and ran up a curtain. There it sat out of sight and mind of the revellers. But if anyone had cared to look upwards they would have seen the little beast peering out from the topmost folds of the curtain, glancing now and then at the fun and frolics of Ireland's leading men and women. For the most part, though, the insect's gaze was fixed on Lady Kirwan as she bowed, danced and exchanged pleasantries.

A couple of nights after the wedding, Lord Kirwan was making ready to go on his honeymoon. The newlyweds would be leaving at daybreak and there was much still to organise. Lord Kirwan sent a servant to enquire after his wife, but his wife was nowhere to be found. The lord then called for his wife's maid and asked where her mistress was.

'I last saw her walking towards kitchen, sir. She told me to retire as it was late. So I did so, sir.'

'Why was she going to the kitchen?'

'The cook had reported a problem, sir and wanted her ladyship's advice.'

Lord Kirwan dismissed the maid and went down to the kitchen. The cook was finishing up as he entered.

'My wife called on you earlier?' he asked. 'You had trouble, I hear?'

'Yes, sir. Most of the staff had finished for the day. There was only me and the boy left. He was finishing the sweeping and I was getting hampers prepared for your journey. Then we heard a scratching and a clattering noise and saw, oh it was awful, hundreds of insects pouring through the back door. The boy turned white with the shock of it. Oh it makes me ill to think of it, beetles, earwigs, ants and saints-know-what other little monsters, all scuttling up the table legs and up on to the stove and everywhere.

'I slammed the hampers shut, sir, and sent the boy to go tell his mistress that I might not be able to get the hampers filled as there was a plague in the kitchen like the one that bedevilled the Egyptians. Well, the boy returned with the mistress and she was all efficiency and unperturbedness, sir. "Nothing a good sweeping and a good cleaning won't fix," she said, sir, without a blink and the beetles scuttling over her shoes as she stood there. Magnificent she was, sir, made orders like a general. Told the boy and me to go fetch wood and water. "We'll boil them," she said, "then sweep out their remains and clean the kitchen from top to bottom. If the three of us work hard it'll be done in no time."

'Well, I did as I was ordered, went with the boy to fetch wood and water, but I did not think it proper that her ladyship should do the work with us. So I went to wake the scullery maid, sir, and then I had to explain what had happened, and then the boy, who was still in a state, shaking like a newborn lamb in a winter storm, well, he spilled the water and had to go fetch more. What with one thing and another it was twenty minutes before we all returned to the kitchen. And what a wonder to see, sir. All the insects were gone and the kitchen spick and span as if nothing had ever happened. Well, I said a prayer of thanks to God that we have been blessed with such an efficient mistress.'

'And what did Lady Kirwan do then?'

'Oh, her ladyship was not in the kitchen, sir. I presumed she had gone to finish her packing, sir.'

Lord Kirwan looked around the clean kitchen. The back door was open and the blackness beyond was deep and terrible. 'Wait here,' he said, and walked slowly to the darkness. With a deep breath and a silent prayer he stepped through the doorway.

No stars lit the sky. No moonlight broke through the thick clouds. The trees could scarcely be seen, reduced to black shapes on a black canvas. Fearful now, the lord almost cried out when something tugged at his sleeve. Looking down, he saw an old woman standing beside him, her face lined with age, her thin body wrapped in filthy rags.

'I have witnessed a crime, sir,' she wailed. 'A terrible crime. Finnbheara himself I've seen this night, riding for Knockma on a great black steed, and the Lady Kirwan thrown on the horse before him like a sack of turnips, sir. You must rescue her, rescue her quick, before the sun rises or she will never be able to leave his palace beneath the hill, sir.'

Lord Kirwan did not hesitate. He sent word to every house within his estate, ordering every man and boy to look out digging tools and come immediately to Knockma. Likewise his own staff were roused from their beds. Valet, butler, coachman and gardener; the boy who polished the shoes and the boy who cleaned the stables, all were roused up and sent out to Knockma. And not a man nor a boy complained once they learned of the terrible blow that had befallen the mistress of Castle Hackett House.

Like an army, the men and boys assembled at the foot of Knockma. Many were fearful, for it was no light thing to make war against immortals, but when the order came, on they marched with pickaxes and shovels to begin the dirty business of hacking into the living soil of Knockma. Within an hour and a half, a massive hole had been dug into the hill. Lord Kirwan ordered a brief rest. The warriors rested, drank water and eagerly vowed Lady Kirwan would be freed before the sun rose. But when they returned to their campaign a terrible confusion assailed them, for the hole that they had dug had vanished.

Lord Kirwan grabbed a pickaxe and attacked the hill again. 'No fairy dare defy me!' roared he, as his weapon rose and fell, rose and fell, and broke up the stone and soil of that devilish hill. Inspired by their leader, and fortified with a shot of brandy, the men and boys set to once more, but to no avail. The new hole they dug was deeper than the last, but the exhaustion was greater. This time they rested only a few minutes, but when they turned again to their assault, the found the second hole had likewise vanished.

The bravery of Lord Kirwan's battalions began to crumble; whispered doubts and fears echoed through the night air. As the mortals faced defeat, Lord Kirwan spied beyond the lights of the lanterns the old ragged woman. She stepped forward and declared, 'Make haste, Lord Kirwan, the sun will rise soon and your wife will be trapped beneath the hill for all eternity.'

'We dig,' explained the weary lord. 'But no matter how deep and wide, the hole fills up again.'

'Fool!' spat the old woman. 'How can you be so lacking in knowledge and your family living here for generations?'

'What is it that I do not know?' asked Lord Kirwan, humbly.

'Salt, my dear,' replied the old woman in a kinder voice. 'Mark with salt the boundary of the place you want to dig up. No magic will be able to stop you then.'

The lord sent his steward to fetch salt. 'Hurry, man,' he ordered. 'The night is growing old.' The steward returned forty minutes later. A boundary was marked out with salt and the call went up again. 'Dig, men! Dig! Dig with no rest. Dig before the sun rises and my wife is lost forever.'

They dug, grunting and sweating, blades breaking the hill, soil clods and stony splinters bursting all around, the air shaking from the ding and crack of this last desperate assault. When the hole was twenty feet wide and twenty feet deep a cry came from the bottom of the pit. 'Stop before you bring my roof in.'

Lord Kirwan scrambled into the hole, the mud as thick and heavy on him as a suit of armour. He bent down and called out, 'Is it yourself, Finnbheara?'

'It is. Now stop your nonsense before you break through the ceiling of my palace.'

'We'll stop if you return my wife.'

'Ah, now, sure she's having a great time here. Dancing, feasting …'

Lord Kirwan raised his pickaxe.

'Stop!' called the king of the Connacht immortals. 'I'll return your wife if you cease digging.'

'Do you give your word?' demanded Lord Kirwan.

'I do,' said Finnbheara.

Lord Kirwan and his little army left the hill and returned in triumph to Castle Hackett House. The young lord made his way to the kitchen to order food and drink for his fine warriors. There, standing in the darkness before the kitchen door, he saw his wife. He grasped her and wept for joy, but his wife did not respond. Kirwan, weighed down with filth and exhaustion, did not realise at first what had befallen his wife. He gave her into the care of her lady's maid and went to clean and refresh himself. When he called into his wife's chamber he saw her sitting on a chair. Beside her stood the maid, her eyes glistening with tears. 'My mistress does not respond,' she whispered. 'She will not speak, eat or sup the wine I offer her.'

Lord Kirwan, fear and anger shivering in his belly, knelt before his wife and kissed her hand. There was no response. Lady Kirwan's expression was blank and her body stiff and motionless. The maid, weeping freely now, declared, 'She is trapped by a spell, sir. Her body is here but her mind is elsewhere. Oh, sir, I fear it is the work of Finnbheara.'

'Don't speak his name,' hissed the lord of Castle Hackett House. Senseless with rage, he ran from the room. Down the stairs and out into the night he went, his only thought to run to Knockma and smash his way through the roof of the palace of the vile fairy king. But his way was barred by the old woman in her rags. 'You will not get there before the sun rises, sir,' said she. 'And by then it will be far too late.'

'What then can I do to save my wife?'

'You must remove the spell.'

'How?'

'There will be a fairy pin on her. Remove the pin and bring it to me. But do it quickly, for the dawn is almost on us.'

Lord Kirwan hurried back to his wife's room and gave quick instruction to the lady's maid. 'There is a pin. It is magic. We must find it and remove it.'

His hands were clumsy as he tugged at the folds of his wife's garments. Less than a minute passed and with a whoop of joy he pulled out a pin. The maid shook her head. 'A lady's attire has many pins, sir. That is one of her own. Let me look, sir. I will know the false pin when I see it.'

The maid slowly and carefully began to examine her mistress's clothes. Lord Kirwan paced the room, looked at the clock, turned to the maid, and bit his tongue. A few more long thin aching minutes stretched by. Lord Kirwan continued pacing back and forth, back and forth, all the while stopping himself from screaming 'Hurry up, you fool!'

Then the maid turned round. 'Here it is, sir.' She smiled and held out her hand, and there was a golden pin as small and sharp as a thorn. The lord laughed, kissed the blushing maid on the top of her head and hurried back down the stairs. Outside the sky was lighter, his estate stretched before him in the pale morning gloom. Speechless he handed the magic pin to the old wrinkled woman. 'Your wife is saved,' said she, 'and just in time.'

Lord Kirwan watched as the sun peeped over the horizon, paused for a moment, then rose in a great red ball of fire. When he looked at the old woman again he saw that he had been joined by a great black horse. As the sun rose higher, so the old woman began to change. Her rags turned to the finest silks, her figure grew taller as her wrinkled skin softened. Soon a tall, beautiful woman stood before the awestruck lord. 'Take care of your spouse, Lord Kirwan,'

she laughed. 'And I'll take care of mine.'
And with that the Lady Oonagh leapt on to
her horse and in a blink she and it vanished
completely.

When Lady Kirwan awoke that afternoon,
she had no memory of what had befallen her.
As for Lord Kirwan, he never again showed
disrespect to the immortal majesties who live
under that magical hill.

11

The Pooka and the Boy

There once was a boy called Finn who, being very poor, was small for his age. He lived in a little house with his mother out in the Galway countryside. There were farms nearby and woodlands, and though the boy was very poor the world around him was filled with a richness of scents, sounds, tastes and textures. The dry roughness of tree bark, the soft song of birds; the impatient rattle of autumn winds; the scent of the dark soil conjured up by the touch of rain in summer.

It was a magical place, though the boy did not understand how truly magical it was. He knew he should never be in the nearby woods alone at night, for that was when the *daoine maithe* and other magical creatures came out to play. Their favourite spot was the rickety wooden bridge that crossed the stream that went through the middle of the woods. Even in bright daylight the bridge was a little spooky; on more than one occasion Finn was sure he had seen strange eyes peering out from the shadows underneath it.

His mother would often leave a little gift for these magical beings outside the back door. Sometimes she put out a thimble of milk, and Finn put beside it a feather he had found, or shiny stone. 'It's not much,' said his mother, 'but it shows our respect.'

Another household ritual took place at meal times, when his mother would ask the boy to leave a little bit of food on his plate as a gift for the Good Folk. She would insist on this, even if he only had a little food on his plate. But he did not complain, for there were evenings when his mother sat at the table with no plate in front of her at all. So Finn left a morsel on his plate, and on those occasions when his mother had no food herself he left more than a morsel, for as he grew older he began to suspect that it was his mother who was eating the portions put aside for the *daoine maithe*.

Indeed, as he grew older Finn began to have doubts about whether strange and fantastical beings truly haunted the woods at night. Perhaps his mother only told him such a thing because she was worried that he could become lost or have an accident in the dark.

The boy was good-natured and helpful. He worked as hard as his mother to clean the house and do piecemeal work in the farms around. But, like all children, he had his wilful streak. One Christmas he went into the local village just before dawn, broke into the priest's house – it helped that he was small enough to squeeze through the open window – and stole the goose that was hanging up in the holy man's kitchen.

At first he felt delighted at his prize but when he got home he felt guilty and ashamed. He also felt foolish, for what could he do with a stolen goose? How could he cook it without his home, upset and unsure of what to do, his his crime being found out? As he stood outside mother came out. She looked at him, looked at the goose, and her eyes sparked with sudden anger. Then, to the boy's amazement, the anger vanished. His mother burst out laughing. 'Would you look at that?' she said. 'The fairies have left *us* a gift this time – how very kind of them.'

The boy tried to tell her the truth but she just laughed more and tousled his hair, and soon the boy found himself laughing as well. The goose was cooked for lunch and it tasted wonderful. He would remember the soft moist creamy taste of it for a long time afterwards. The goose incident convinced him once and for all that there was no such things as fairies. That was, of course, until the night he met a pooka.

A pooka, for those who do not know, is a magical shapeshifter who can bring good fortune or ill depending on how it is feeling and how it is treated. There are many in the west of Ireland where Finnbheara and Oonagh are the rulers of the fairy kingdom. But it is hard to say whether pookas recognise the authority of these immortal majesties. Being tricksters, they are not known for straight talking (I have tried talking to one myself and, believe me, it was an incredibly frustrating business). They may have arrived in Ireland with the angels who were cast out of Heaven, or they may have already have been here. They could even have been in Ireland a long, long, *fadó fadó* ago when the Cailleach was hammering the mountains, rivers and coastlines into shape with her hammer.

But, I hear you ask, how did Finn come to meet a pooka, and what came of this encounter? Well, it's like this. As I was explaining, Finn and his mother were very poor and often hungry. There were a number of heirlooms that could have been sold for a fair bit of money, but Finn's mother refused: 'These are our heritage, no price can be put on them.' One of these heirlooms was a set of uillean pipes that had belonged to Finn's grandfather. Finn found the instrument fascinating and would often take it out to press the bellows or blow a peep from the chanter.

But it was only after he turned ten years of age that he began to think about playing the pipes himself. His grandfather had made money travelling around playing his tunes. Why shouldn't Finn do the same?

'I will be a piper,' he declared to his mother. 'I will be the greatest piper that ever lived and make us rich.'

His mother though for a moment. 'I have a cousin married to a man that plays the pipes a little,' she said. 'If you help them out with the turf cutting I'm sure he'll give you a few lessons.'

An arrangement was made and Finn began his lessons, but there was a problem. Finn wanted so desperately to be a piper, the greatest piper that ever lived no less, that he did not have the patience to listen to his instructor. 'Some say it takes a year to learn,' his tutor explained. 'Some say twenty-one years or more. But the truth is, Finn, that you never finish learning.'

'Never finish!' the boy blurted out. 'That is terrible.'

'Not at all. That is the joy of playing the pipes. Once you get to know your pipes, you will fall in love with them and dream about them every night you sleep and every moment you walk and wake and work. Because you love them you will always be looking for new tunes to play or new techniques to try with them. You will never finish learning and you will always want to know more.'

But Finn did not want to spend a lifetime learning. He wanted to play the pipes and play them *now*, this minute, this second, and play them better than any man, woman or child had ever played them.

His mother's cousin's husband's instructions made Finn ever more irate.

'The secret is simplicity itself,' explained the tutor. 'While your upper arms do the hard work with the bellows and bag, your fingers play lightly on the chanter. Practise slowly and practise often to do this, and then we can start playing tunes.'

Seeing the doubt in Finn's eyes, his tutor assured him. 'Treat the pipes with kindness and patience and you will be rewarded with beauty and peace.'

But Finn had no patience. Instead he grappled and fought the uillean pipes, like a wrestler in a circus pounding his opponent into submission, or an Amazon explorer struggling heroically against the mighty coils of a savage boa constrictor. Instead of loving the pipes, he waged war against them. His instructor shook his head and advised him that 'The pipes need peace and patience. That's the way to get them playing.' But the boy's anger and stubbornness grew with every lesson until finally with a roar he ran out from one, vowing never to return.

It was daylight when Finn ran outside. He ran and ran until there was no more breath to be squeezed out of his lungs. He stood gasping for air with the pipes clenched against his body and his eyes clenched against any tears. When he calmed down he looked around. The day was bright and he had nothing to do. He should have gone home to his mother to help her in her chores, but he did not want to explain what had happened at his lesson.

Instead, he took himself for a walk. He wandered along the edge of fields of barley, scratched the noses of cows in meadows, threw stones at crows and picked apples from an orchard. He sat down now and then to enjoy the sun. His instrument rested beside him and sometimes he would look at it or touch it lightly. 'Will I ever become a piper?' he asked, but the uillean pipes were silent. Perhaps they were too busy enjoying the sunshine.

The day went on but the boy, carefree and smiling, took no heed of the lengthening shadows. Eventually the sun decided to go to bed just as Finn was stepping into the woods that led to his mother's house. The boy did not want to delay his return home any longer, for that would worry his mother. 'It's light enough yet. I'll stick to the path and be home soon enough.' He was a little nervous – 'not because of fairies, oh no, they don't exist' – just because he had never been in the woods at night before. But he was not afraid; the evening was warm and sweet smelling; birds were singing evening songs, and there were no such things as fairies and magical creatures, oh no.

The darkness deepened, though, and whatever light there was fled. It was harder to see the path in front of him. Finn began to worry more than a little bit. When he heard the sound of the stream he felt relieved and scared at the same time. Relieved because finding the stream would mean that he was halfway home and still on the path; but that path led not only to the stream but also to the rickety wooden bridge where, so his mother had assured him, all manner of strange and terrible nocturnal creatures congregated.

On the boy walked. The sound of the water trickling grew louder, as did the crunch and crackle of his footsteps upon the woodland path. Soon he saw the bridge, lit up by starlight. It glowed in the darkness like a ghost, while beneath it was a blackness that seemed to move and breathe as if alive – alive and waiting. Finn's feet moved more slowly. He clenched the pipes more tightly. It was only a bridge; that was all. If he ran he would be over faster than any fairy or demon from Hell could reach out of the shadows and snatch him. Seconds it would take him. Only seconds and he'd be across to the other side and if he kept on running, sure he'd be home in ten minutes or less.

He walked cautiously, the path crackling beneath his feet. Closer and closer he came to that awful ramshackle crossing. His mind was made up now. He would stop, take a deep breath and then, whoosh, he would race across it. He stopped walking, but oh how terrible! Though he had stopped moving he could still hear a crackling and crunching sound. Eyes wide, he stared down, but his feet were perfectly still. Something else was moving on the path behind him. Raising his pipes like a weapon, he turned round. There stood a skinny goat with huge horns on its head.

Finn screamed in terror; he turned back to the bridge and in an explosion of energy shot forward. Nearer and nearer the glowing frame of the bridge came; brighter and brighter it glowed and beamed like a white fire or a burning frost. So terrible it was that he closed his eyes even as his feet pounded on to its creaking, shifting, shaking frame that seemed to go on and on and on. 'Nearly there,' the boy gasped. 'Nearly there.'

Then he smacked full force into something. He bounced backwards and fell on his back. Shocked, he opened his eyes and saw, there on the bridge in front of him, the very same goat. It too glowed in the starlight. But worse by far was the way the creature looked at the boy; scrutinising him with an awful alien intelligence.

Finn, trembling with fear, knew then that this was not an ordinary goat; this was a pooka, a magical shapeshifting trickster that could do him great harm. But the creature's gaze softened as if satisfied with what it saw. And then it spoke.

'Howya?' the pooka said, with a wink. 'Would they be your own pipes that you're clinging on to for dear life?'

The trembling boy nodded his head.

'How good are you?'

Finn sat up. He was scared, but no longer shocked. His sense of fear had faded, to be replaced by a sense of wonder. It was all true, all the stories his mother had told him about the magical creatures who walked the woods in the evening. Staring back at the goat he declared in a shaky voice, 'I am the best piper in all of Ireland.'

'Is that so,' smirked the pooka. 'Play me a tune then.'

Brave as he was stubborn, the boy determined to show this talking goat that even though he was small he feared nothing. He grabbed his pipes, furrowed his brow in concentration, flexed his fingers and set to with a mighty vigour. But oh, what a cacophony squealed and parped and screeched from the chanter! It was a sound like a thousand constipated cats meowling in pain while simultaneously farting in frustration.

The boy stopped with a gasp. He stared at the pooka as if challenging it to make a comment. But the magic goat merely shrugged. 'Mmm,' it mused. 'You may need a little help there.' So saying, it shook its head violently and a blast of sparks spurted out from the tips of its razor-sharp horns. Finn braced himself as the sparks, glowing like embers, covered him and his pipes. But the little lights did not burn. They merely touched the boy and his instrument and instantly vanished.

'Try again,' insisted the pooka.

Finn did as he was asked, but this time the result was very different. The instrument felt lighter and the boy more relaxed. Bellow and bag rose and fell beneath his elbows easy and untroubled. His fingers were more supple and assured, almost as if the chanter was guiding them gaily up and down its frame. Instead of an ugly racket, a sweet tune skipped out of the instrument playful and joyous.

'Grand so,' nodded the pooka. 'Now, quick, follow me before my guests start complaining.'

Finn, still playing a wonderful tune, followed the goat as it trip-tropped over the bridge and then squeezed through a dense thicket of leaves and twigs. Finn stopped playing and pushed his way through the vegetation. Twigs scratched and leaves flapped but on he went until pop! he burst out the other side and discovered he

was in a plain wooden hall, thickly packed with laughing and singing revellers. As the pooka shouted out, 'Make way there!' a narrow gap appeared in the middle of the crowd. The boy looked and to his amazement saw the strangest and most terrifying party-goers he had ever encountered. There were cackling witches here and wafting ghosts there. Skeletons rattled their bones and just in front of him, was that the spirit of the goose he had stolen last Christmas?!

Soon the cry went up, 'Here's the piper!' The pooka waited for the boy to catch up with him then whispered in his ear. 'Don't be afraid. They're in a good mood, but don't take any food or drink they offer you. Just play a few tunes and then I'll get you home again safe and sound.'

'You promise?' whispered the boy.

'Well, let's just say I'll promise to try and get you safely home again.' With that the goat cut off the conversation by banging a hoof loudly on the floor. A stool appeared beside him and the hellish crowd grew quiet. Finn sat on the stool and picked up his pipes. The pooka smiled and winked at him. The brave and stubborn boy closed his eyes and began playing.

The tunes danced and jigged out of the chanter, and the boy's fingers danced and jigged with them, while his feet tapped time and his arms moved to the breathing of the bellows and bag. Even the skraiching of the witches did not distract him from his playing. He only took one glance at his audience, but quickly looked back to his instrument for what he briefly glimpsed was horrifying indeed. All around the hall magical beings danced and leapt while filling the air with blood-curdling screeches. Finn closed his eyes and played on, with each tune faster and wilder than the one before.

When he stopped to take a breath, the pooka banged the floor again. 'Time to pay the piper,' he cried. Sure enough, all those erlish creatures stopped their mad cavorting and formed an orderly queue. One by one they thanked the boy and handed him a golden penny. When the last creature – the ghost of the Christmas goose – dropped its penny in Finn's hand the pooka hissed, 'Now follow me, boy, as quick as you can, before my guests change their mind.'

Through the crowd the pooka and boy went. They pushed open a door and squeezed through a thick hedge. The boy tumbled out of the hedge and found himself back in the woods, on the path that led from the bridge to his mother's house. '*Slan abhaile*,' said the pooka with a crooked smile and a dangerous wink. Then the creature vanished and the boy was alone in the dark woods. Terrified that a witch or a skeleton might leap out and snatch him, he began to run as fast as his short legs could take him.

Through the front door of his house he burst, and fell exhausted and weeping in front of his mother. 'Thank God,' she said, helping him up and hugging him close. 'I was so worried when you had not come home.'

'I'm so sorry Mother, I didn't believe you. I went into the woods after dark and everything you said was true.' He told her the whole story and when he finished put his hand in his pocket. 'I'm not lying, Mother. Look, here are the gold coins.' But when he open his hands there were only hazelnuts there.

His mother took one of the hazelnuts and quietly examined it. 'You're very lucky,' she said, quietly. 'They only played a trick on you. It could have been far worse. Let's hope you've brought no magic back with you.'

'But what about my pipes,' wailed Finn. 'They had magic on them and I played them better than any piper that has ever lived.' With that he sat on a chair, made his instrument ready and began to play. But the magic was gone and the sound was awful, almost as bad on the ears as the screeching of the witches. Finn refused to believe he could not play. Harder he banged away at the bellows, tighter he gripped and pounded at the chanter. His mother called on him to cease his racket, but angry and upset the boy carried on louder and louder until the whole countryside was woken by his pipes as they wailed and screamed like a body being murdered.

From near and far the neighbours came racing, banging at the door and then pushing their way in. At the front was the priest, his eyes blazing as he pointed at the boy and demanded he cease in the name of God and the martyrs.

Well, that crowd had no sympathy for a small boy in torment. They booed and catcalled and called him terrible names. But he would not be beaten down by anybody else's opinions. He was stubborn and brave, but also clever and wise. Even as the noise of his detractors shook the tiles from the roof, the boy paused. He remembered the advice that the husband of the cousin of his mother had given him. Treat the pipes with kindness and patience.

Finn took a breath and found a quiet stillness inside him. 'I don't need magic,' he told himself. Slowly he began playing again. This time the pipes responded to his gentle coaxing, and to the boy's delight a simple tune drifted out from the chanter. The notes were soft and quiet but something about the manner of the boy caught the attention of his annoyed neighbours. Gone was his angry frown; his hands were no longer bunched up like fists. He looked calm and at ease. He looked, in fact, like a piper.

The crowd fell quiet. 'Keep playing,' said his mother. Finn did so but only for a little while.

He was tired and it was late. But for the ten minutes or so that he played the neighbours smiled and tapped their feet in appreciation. When Finn finished playing every man, woman and member of the clergy there clapped and cheered. And that, boys and girls, is the story of how Finn began his life as a world-famous piper.

12

The White Trout

There once was a soldier wounded in body and soul, who fled from battle. In time he came to live in the country between Knockma and Cong. He built a simple shack in the woods and there he settled.

Word of his arrival spread quickly and visitors came calling, many offering advice and help. A small bed, a stove, a table and two chairs were donated to him. The soldier thanked people for their gifts, but it was noted that he did not smile and he did not invite people into his home. Wounded in body and soul, the soldier struggled to keep his anger at bay. He felt safer on his own.

But there was one man called Padraig who persisted in coming round. The soldier refused to invite him into his simple home and spoke only a few words to him. But Padraig was patient. One morning he turned up at the soldier's door carrying a rod and line. He also brought a piece of advice: 'You can eat well here and clear your head at the same time.'

'Is that so?' said the soldier.

'The river is filled with trout at this time of the year. In fact it's so full that some of the poor fishes would welcome a change of scenery. You would be doing them a favour if you caught them, cooked them and put them in your belly.'

The angry soldier went to close his door but Padraig stuck his foot in and said, 'Nothing beats fishing on a clear day with the sound of the birds above you and the splash of the river before you.'

Padraig pushed the rod and line through the door. The soldier looked at the long, thin pole. He had never fished in his life and was not sure what to make of the contraption. However, his life as a soldier had taught him that ignorance was dangerous. It was important that a man understood how things worked. Lack of knowledge could very easily lead to a lack of blood or limbs, or even life itself.

The soldier opened the door. 'Please show me how it works.'

'Gladly. My name is Padraig.' Padraig held out his hand.

'I am Eisa,' said the soldier as they shook hands.

The two men walked along a trail through the woods. Insects buzzed and birds sang boastful songs. The trees were draped in greens and between the leaves sunlight glinted like jewellery. Soon they came to a river that was not so big but big enough and deep enough. The bottom of the river was lined with soft-edged stones, reds and browns, greys and blacks, all polished up like boots on a parade ground.

Padraig sat on the river bank and pointed. 'Look there.' Eisa looked and saw something move in the shaded part of the water. The shape

 darted into sunlight, then another joined it and another.

The wounded soldier smiled. 'These fish have stripes like little tigers.'

'They're trout,' explained Padraig. 'Now sit down beside me and I'll show you how to catch them.'

By the end of the day the wounded soldier was as proficient with rod and line as ever he had been with gun and blade. Together the men caught a dozen fish. As they walked back towards Eisa's simple home, Padraig said, 'Will I show you how to cook them?'

The wounded soldier nodded. 'Yes, thank you.'

In the little shack Padraig showed the wounded soldier how to gut and clean the fish. Then while butter melted in a large pan, he rolled each fish in flour, salt and pepper. When the butter was bubbling he placed two of the trout in. Five minutes later they were ready for eating. 'Delicious,' grinned Eisa. 'Delicious to eat and delicious to smell.' And that was how Padraig became the first person made welcome into the home of the wounded soldier.

Over the weeks the two men went fishing every other day. At first Padraig was curious about Eisa. Did he have family? What was his home country like? But Eisa would not talk about such things and Padraig asked no more. The two men spoke little, both content to take in the sounds, scents and colours of the woods and the water.

One day they followed the trail a little further along from their usual fishing spot. They came to a place where the river widened into a deep pool.

'The trees are thicker here,' explained Padraig, sitting down by the pool. 'There's more shade, which keeps this spot cooler in the summer and shields it from the worst of the winds in the winter. A perfect spot.'

'It's lovely,' agreed Eisa, unwrapping his rod and line.

'People don't fish here,' said Padraig. 'It's more a place for sitting and thinking.'

'But look!' cried Eisa. 'Over there is a huge trout. See, it's white. It's big enough to feed me for a week.'

Padraig laughed and looked up at his friend. 'Ah now, nobody tries to catch the white trout. Shall I tell you why?'

Eisa sat down and continued to get his rod and line ready. His companion gently put his hand on the fishing equipment. 'Listen, Eisa.'

'A long time ago there was a king who ruled these parts. His daughter was kind, clever and witty. She also knew her own heart and told her father she was determined that she would marry only for love and never for politics. The king, who loved his daughter very much, agreed to this.

'Now, from when she was a child the princess would come to this very spot to bathe and rest. She was attended by three handmaidens at the pool, and beyond the trees were posted grim guards. The pool was her place and as private as her own bedchamber. And when the princess became a young woman, the pool became even more important to her as a place to reflect and consider the life before her.

'In time the princess fell in love with the son of a rival king. Despite their history the two monarchs agreed that their children should marry. There was great hope that the marriage would bring an end to conflict in the land.

'On the morning of her wedding the princess came to her beautiful pool to bathe. It was a hot day of shimmering sunlight and the princess delighted in cooling her limbs in the fresh clean water. But the sound of uproar beyond the trees interrupted her. Quickly she dried and dressed while one of her handmaidens went to ask the guards what was happening.

'As she was combing her hair, the handmaiden returned. With her there were two guards. Between the two guards stumbled a man, his face so distraught and soaked with tears and grime that for a moment the princess did not recognise him. Then she realised it was the servant of her

beloved prince. In that very instant she knew the man she loved was dead. She would never see her prince again. Never again hold him in her arms, or listen to his great plans and his soft laughter. He was gone from her and all that they had planned together: adventures, children, old age and shared sorrows and joys. All gone.

'The servant wailed that his master had been killed by assassins on his morning walk. He said much more, but the princess did not hear him. Her strength fell out of her and she collapsed on the bank of this beautiful pool.'

Padraig paused for a moment. The green leaves shifted and sighed like an ocean. Indifferent to the world's sorrows, sunlight and shadow played on the water and on the grassy bank. 'Go on,' demanded the wounded soldier irritably.

'The princess grieved,' continued Padraig. 'There was no end to her grief. Days and years passed but her sorrow only sharpened. Every day she walked with her three handmaidens to this pool. But she would not bathe there.

Instead she demanded of the water: "Where is my betrothed? Where is my husband to be?"

'The princess was loved by the people of the realm, and by her handmaidens and father. But as time passed, love was tempered by impatience. People die all the time, some complained. The princess must allow her wound to heal over, said others. It was disrespectful for her to be so focused on the death of her beloved that she failed to celebrate his life. She was young yet and would love again. The king needed grandchildren and it was selfish of her to not look for a new husband.

'But grief is a personal thing, and there is no right way or wrong way of suffering it.

'Sometimes when she stood by the pool the princess would try to talk to her handmaidens of her lost love, of his laughter and his eyes, but the words would catch in her throat like a hook and she could not speak them.

'Her handmaidens talked among themselves about their mistress. "She would be better off dead," snapped one. "Better if she were fully alive," said another. "If only she would bathe in the pool again," spoke the third, quietly. "Perhaps the water would wash the grief off her."

'Her companions agreed with her, but though they thought and thought and talked and talked, they could not come up with a plan for getting the princess to bathe in the pool. Finally in despair all the silly maidens whispered at the same time, "Oh, I wish our princess would bathe in the pool again."

'And so that's what happened. The next day they accompanied the mourning princess to the pool. But again the princess refused to bathe. She stood staring at the water and demanded: "Where is my betrothed? Where is my husband to be?" Just then a loud rustling alarmed the handmaidens. They looked towards the trees but there was nothing there. When they turned back, the princess was gone. The maidens searched and the guards searched, but nothing was found of her on the riverbank or in the woods. Then the men and women searched the pool. And there they saw a large trout, its body as white as a wedding gown, and they knew that their mistress had been transformed.

'There the white trout has remained to this day. Some say she is waiting for her beloved prince yet. Others say that she is waiting for all the grief to be washed from her, for only then can she join her prince in Heaven. And others say the trout is just a trout, though large and white and long living.'

Padraig smiled at his companion, but the wounded soldier's face was dark with anger. Snatching up his rod and line the wounded soldier hissed, 'I am not a fool that you can trick and taunt with fairy tales.' With that Eisa hurried along the trail and back to his shack. There he stayed all day, refusing to open the door when Padraig knocked on it. Wounded in body and soul the soldier struggled to keep his anger at bay. Padraig eventually stopped knocking and left. Eisa paced the floor of his small home, his anger growing brighter and fiercer until he knew what he must do. He would go that very night and catch the white trout. Catch it, kill it, cook it and eat it.

Late in the evening Eisa made his way back to the pool. Above the branches and leaves of the trees stars blinked. It was a cool night and beautiful but Eisa thought only of the white trout and how he would soon slaughter it. When he came to the pool he saw the water was as black as the night sky. The fish floated lazily in the darkness, its whiteness glowing like a dream. Eisa, calmer now, attached a hook to the line. On the hook a worm wriggled. Eisa cast his line and waited. He waited a long time but the fish showed no interest. It simply swam in a slow, wide circle.

Frustrated, the wounded soldier threw aside his rod and stepped into the night-black pool. 'I'll catch you with my own hands,' he muttered, and began to wade towards the fish. As he walked the pool got deeper until the cold water was up to the wounded soldier's waist. Shivering, he looked around and to his surprise saw that the fish was only two or three feet from him. The creature was no longer swimming in a circle, but floated in one spot just beneath the surface of the water. It was much larger by far than any other trout Eisa had seen over the summer. Larger and cleverer, for it seemed to be watching him.

As Eisa stepped closer to the curious beast he remembered Padraig talking about how when he was a boy he caught fish by tickling them. Eisa reached his hand out and put it in the water below the fish and gently stroked its belly. The fish blinked lazily and Eisa was sure its expression changed. 'Did you just smile, my dear?' he cooed softly to the creature. He

stepped closer, all the while stroking the fish's belly. Then he leapt at the creature. Too late it tried to escape. It pounded the water with its powerful tail, twisted and writhed in the snare of the soldier's arms. But Eisa held fast even when he slipped beneath the water. Gagging and choking, he held on to the massive heavy beast, and soon enough he made it back to dry land.

He ran through the woods, clothes heavy and sodden, his arms aching as he held tight on to the gowping, flapping creature. He got into the shack and threw the fish to the floor. The creature's tail whipped side to side, almost knocking the wounded soldier over. But nothing could stop him now. The stove was lit, the butter placed in a large pan, the gutting knife picked up.

Eisa bent down by the large writhing fish. He grabbed its head and brought the knife slicing down. The fish, frantic with fear, twisted aside. The knife cut the fish but did not kill it. Again and again the wounded soldier brought the knife down, but now the creature writhed and twisted so fast and so frantic that no more blows landed on it. 'I'll cook you alive then,' roared Eisa. With that he grabbed the giant fish and threw it into the pan.

The fish screamed and leapt from the pan. And as it screamed and as it leapt the horrified Eisa saw it change, change from a fish into a young woman robed in white, who landed in a heap on the floor before him. Shaking and dumbfounded, Eisa dropped the knife. The woman struggled to her feet. She stood before Eisa with tears in her eyes and a terrible ragged wound on her breast. 'Throw me back,' she moaned. 'Throw me back before I bleed to death.'

And Eisa did so. He shook off the killing madness and, praying to God for forgiveness, he gently lifted the woman. He ran through the darkness, weighed down by the woman and his own grief. The night was dark and his burden heavy, but he did not slip, not even once. Soon he reached the pond where he gently lowered the woman into the water. Instantly she turned

back into the white trout. The wound in its side closed up and healed, leaving only a red mark. With a splash the creature swam down into the darkest part of the pond.

There is little more to say about the wounded soldier and the white trout, but say it I will.

Padraig found his friend the next day, lying by the pool. His clothes were damp and stained with blood. He took him back to his shack and cleaned him up and put him to bed, where he slept for two solid days.

What Eisa dreamt during those days nobody knows, but when he awoke his simmering anger was gone. He remained a quiet man but the quietness had a reflective, curious quality, as if Eisa were noticing the world anew and was humbled by what he saw. He admitted to his friend that he had tried to catch the fish and vowed never to do so again.

The years rolled by. Padraig and Eisa walked, occasionally talked, caught fish and visited the pool of the white trout. If Padraig noticed the red mark on the fish he did not say. For a long time the white trout remained wary of Eisa. It would hide in the shadows whenever he came by. But gradually the fish let go its fear and began swimming in its usual lazy contented fashion.

Eisa had a knack for making and fixing things (a good survival skill for a soldier, and an even better social skill for one living in rural Ireland) and he made a little money as the local handyman. He also made friendly acquaintances. He was happy enough and even developed a droll sense of humour. It was noticeable, though, that he never spoke about his previous life to anyone. At least not to anyone who walked on two legs and lived on dry land.

Sometimes when Padraig went for a walk by himself he would come across Eisa sitting at the pool's edge. His friend would be talking to the white trout, but Padraig made a point of not listening. He would make a lot of noise to alert his friend, and call out a cheery 'hello'.

Eisa lived a long life and I think a happy one. But, as God intended, we are all mortal and in time Eisa's journey in this world finished and the old grey-haired former soldier died. His funeral was packed out and filled with joy and laughter.

Afterwards Padraig went for a walk in the woods. He was ancient now himself and walked slowly between two of his great-grandchildren.

They came to the pool and one of the children asked, 'Where is the white trout?' But the white trout had gone and was never seen again.

For my part I like to think that Eisa and the princess travelled to Heaven together. There, I have no doubt, they met again with the loved ones they had once lost a long, long time ago.

13

The Three Spouses

On the furthest western fringes of the kingdom of Connacht there lies a place called Renvyle. Watched over by brooding mountains, Renvyle is a landscape of large and small hillocks rolling towards the sea like a fleet of homesick whales. The Atlantic spray and gusting rain are ignited into glittering diamonds by the darts of sunlight breaking through the clouds. Not that Renvyle is wet all the time. There are times when the sea and sky are settled, with the waters calm and green and the heavens blue and at ease, and the world around a perfect painting of nature and beauty.

But it is at night that Renvyle is at its most pretty. On clear nights the moon shines like a great ancient coin fallen from the back pocket of the cosmos and stars are scattered like silver drops weaved into the gauzy fabric of the Milky Way.

It was on one such night that a man, who we will call Jack Mhor, was walking down a lonely country road, making his way home from a funeral. The road was lined with thorny hedgerows and the crisp air carried the faint smell of honeysuckle and mud and warm cow dung. His way was lit by the silvery light of the stars and moon, and by this light he saw, a little in front of him, a shape in the middle of the road. Jack Mhor was not sure whether it was a bag of groceries or perhaps a small bundle of rags. But as he drew closer he could see the details of the shape more clearly. To Jack Mhor's surprise the shape was not a bag, nor a bundle, nor even a ball. It was in fact a head, sat there in the road with it eyes open and unmoving.

'Now then,' spoke Jack Mhor, kneeling down. 'Is that not a peculiar affair? A head in a road in want of a body.' He scratched his chin, looked up at the stars for an answer and, getting none, looked back down. The head was still there. 'Well, you are a handsome fellow and that is no mistake. But what a tragedy for a man's top and torso to be estranged from one another. Did you roll out the coffin, I wonder, just before the final box was lowered down?'

So saying, Jack Mhor lifted up the head. 'Well, friend, let's take you to the graveyard and find where your body is settled. Then, God willing, we can effect a reconciliation.'

Holding the head firmly, Jack stood up and turned back the way he had come. To his surprise he saw standing there in the road a figure. It was tall and dressed in an elegant long black coat, topped by a gap where a head should be. The figure held out its arms and Jack Mhor handed it the head. The being took the head and stuck it on to its neck. There was a little bit of twisting and tugging and pulling but soon enough body and head where in perfect harmony. The head opened its mouth, stretched its jaw, closed its mouth, puckered its lips, and then smiled.

Now encountering a head is one thing, but meeting its body up and as active as you and me is a worrisome thing. Indeed it was more than worry that began to shudder its way through Jack Mhor. He hoped – and silently prayed – that the being in front of him was a ghost, as ghosts are harmless enough and more to be pitied than feared. But the being was too solid, too in the world, as it were, to be a mere wraith. No, there was no doubt that Jack Mhor stood before a far more substantial and dangerous creature, nothing less than one of the *daoine maithe*, the good people, the immortals.

The tall man smiled at Jack. 'It's good to see someone capable of showing proper respect due a head. Others have not been so proper. But they were suitably dealt with. Now, please, follow me. I have something to show you.'

The creature turned around and began walking towards the nearby graveyard. Jack, his worries deepening into fear, followed. He had no doubts now that he was in the company of a fairy, and a powerful one at that. It would not do to offend the creature, and yet Jack knew to be on his guard against tricks and deceptions that could see him snatched from this world. What were the rules he had learned as a child? Never eat the food of the good people nor sip their wine. Never listen to their music. Never make them angry. Treat them with absolute respect.

Jack followed the tall gentleman along the road, and as they walked the night grew darker as clouds swallowed the stars. Soon Jack was stumbling in thick blackness. He would have done himself an injury were it not for the fact that a faint light glowed from the figure of the man in front of him, as if the fairy were wearing a cape of moonlight.

Soon Jack found himself in the graveyard. The fairy lord, for Jack had no doubt that he was in the company of magical aristocracy, was standing beside a long gravestone that lay on the ground. The fairy lord bent and gripped one edge of the stone. With a ripping noise he tore it loose from the ground, revealing a deep hole. Beetles, as large and angry as a man's fist, scuttered and clicked out from the hole.

Jack shook as he looked at the great gap in the ground that gaped like a giant mouth hungry for a meal of meat and bone.

'Let's go,' said the fairy in a cheery voice. He clicked his fingers and the hole was filled with a soft light. By this glow Jack could see the beetles lining up in ranks as if they were an army awaiting orders from their commander in chief. The fairy stepped into the gaping hole and began to descend the stairs inside. By now Jack's curiosity was as great as his fear, and his curiosity, let's be honest, was fuelled partly by greed. It was not unheard of for fairies to give gifts to human visitors. Perhaps there was gold down there or some other marvels that would change Jack's life for ever?

With a nod to the insect army, Jack Mhor stepped into the open grave. Carefully he followed the narrow stairs down and down. He came at last to a long corridor made of dark rich soil woven through with pale strands of roots, and lit by a dull glow. There stood the fairy lord, a thoughtful expression on his handsome face.

'Look down the length of the corridor,' he said. 'Tell me what you see.'

Jack looked at the corridor stretching before him and after a few minutes noticed something. 'There are three long shallow indents in the right-hand wall.' As he looked the indents began to change. 'They're becoming doors,' cried Jack Mhor with excitement, as he thought of gold and of treasure.

'Good.' The fairy smiled. 'Let's go take a closer look. There may be things of value here, what think you, mortal?'

Jack said nothing as he and the fairy walked to the door farthest away. 'Open it,' commanded the fairy and Jack Mhor eagerly did so.

What he saw was a most curious thing. For the door opened on to a plain-looking kitchen with a stove in one corner and a window in the other. In the middle of the room was a table covered in scratches and stains. Standing before the stove was a figure.

'This,' whispered the fairy, 'is the first spouse. Watch closely.'

The figure at the stove turned round. It was a woman carrying a great pot filled with potatoes. What she wore, or the colour of her hair, or any other details, escaped Jack Mhor, for he was so startled by the expression on the woman's face. There was such anger and bitterness in her expression it seemed as if the very lines on her face were etched into a hieroglyph of rage and hatred.

'Here's your supper!' screamed the woman as she slammed the pot on the table. 'Eat it! It's all we have, you wretch, you fool, you lazy, pathetic …'

The fairy closed the door on the scene. In the quiet he looked down at Jack Mhor. 'The woman you have just seen was poor all of her life. It made her bitter and angry, and though she died a long time ago she remains angry and bitter yet, with no hope of peace or contentment. Now open the second door and let's see the second spouse.'

Jack Mhor took a breath and obeyed the fairy (for who would dare disobey such a creature?).

The door opened to reveal another kitchen, with a stove in one corner and a window in the other, and there in the middle a table scratched and stained. Standing before the stove was a figure.

'This,' whispered the fairy, 'is the second spouse. Watch closely.'

The figure at the stove turned round. It was a man carrying a great pot filled with potatoes that were burnt and ruined. What he wore, or the colour of his hair, or any other details, escaped Jack Mhor, for he was so startled by the expression on the man's face. His eyes were red rimmed and teary, but his mouth was twisted into a snarl.

This second spouse slammed the pot on the table. Some of the charred potatoes fell out. 'Here's your lovely supper,' he hissed, his voice dripping with sarcasm and bitterness. 'It's all we have in the world and I've worked on it all day, so eat it, you fool, you wastrel, you …'

The fairy closed the door and said: 'The second spouse lived in poverty too. It made him bitter and spiteful, and though he died long ago, he remains bitter and spiteful yet. Now, let's open the last door and observe the third spouse.'

Jack Mhor opened the third door. Again he looked on a kitchen, with a stove in one corner and a window in the other. In the middle was a table, its age-blackened surface gleaming like a mirror. At the stove stood a figure. When it turned round Jack Mhor felt his heart grow light. He was looking at a woman who radiated peace and love. Her clothes were plain, to be sure, and showed signs of constant mending, but her face was handsome and her eyes strong and kind. She smiled as she spoke: 'It's potatoes again for supper, but there are far worse things in the world.' She placed a mat on the table and then put the pot carefully on the mat. She cut up some butter and put it on the potatoes, then sprinkled on some chopped chives and black peppercorn. 'Fit for royalty,' she said with a laugh. 'Let's eat.'

Jack Mhor made to step into the room. He was suddenly filled with an aching hunger for food and the company of this lovely woman. But the fairy held him back. 'Wait a moment.'

As they watched, the woman stopped moving. All the kitchen was filled with stillness. Even the steam rising off the golden potatoes became still. It was as if the scene had become some great painting. But then the picture began to change. The plain clothes on the woman began to fill out and brighten until she was wearing a great silk gown trimmed with gold lace and glints of sapphire. Upon the woman's head there appeared a silver crown that glittered and sparkled as a great light began to fill the room. The light grew brighter and brighter, swallowing the table, the pot, the stove and then the woman herself. Jack Mhor cried out as in pain and struggled against the fairy's iron grip. But the creature simply closed the door and Jack Mhor slumped down.

'The third spouse,' explained the fairy, 'lived in great poverty. But she found happiness and joy where she could, and shared that joy and happiness with all around her. And when she died she was clothed in fine apparel and jewels and taken to reside in the great happiness of the world beyond this.'

The magical being touched the door as if he too yearned to step through. But the door vanished and all that was left was a slight indent in the dark soil.

The fairy turned to Jack Mhor. 'Let's go,' he said wistfully. 'I have a terrible hunger on me.'

They made their way back up the stairs, but when he stepped out into the night, Jack discovered they were no longer in a darkened graveyard. He stood instead on the soft neatly trimmed lawn of a great garden. Above him the sky was filled with the blaze of a million sparkling stars. By their illumination he could see that the garden was bordered on three sides by woods. On the fourth side of the garden stood a magnificent mansion with turrets on the roof and a columned portico leading to its front door. The windows of the magnificent house were filled with the movement of golden light and sable shadow as if a great throng of people were moving within, and the sound of laughter was clearly audible.

'We are just in time,' said the fairy noble. 'My guests have arrived. Shall we go in?'

Jack Mhor had no doubt now that he was in the company of one of the most powerful of the immortal beings. A mistake now and he would never return to his home and friends and family. Yet what to do? He must not attend the party, but likewise he must not offend the fairy.

'Thank you, sir,' he said politely. 'It is very gracious of you to invite me in. But before I do so, may I have a moment to myself? I feel I need to think on what you kindly showed me in the graveyard.'

'Of course,' smiled the fairy and with great elegance he sat himself upon the grass. Jack sat down beside him. 'There is no hurry,' explained the fairy. 'We have all the time in the world. But would you mind if I ordered some food, as I have a terrible hunger on me.'

Before Jack replied, the being snapped his fingers and two servants appeared, each carrying a great tray heavy with foods and drink. The figures bowed to the fairy then knelt down. They unfolded a silken cloth, and placed on it many foodstuffs. There were meats and sauces, cooked vegetables and bowls of fruit, freshly baked loaves and pastries. Jack turned his gaze from the feast, but his stomach gurgled and his mouth watered as he breathed in scents of garlic and basil, of cinnamon and freshly baked bread.

'Eat,' whispered the fairy. 'You know you want to.'

'I would,' spluttered poor Jack, 'but the food is too rich for me.'

'Then try something simple,' said the fairy, and offered Jack a great green and shiny apple. The fairy stretched out on the grass and looked up at the great candelabra of stars overhead. 'Bring music,' he ordered the servants, then closed his eyes.

Jack looked at the globe in his hand and thought how delicious it looked. Yet he managed to force himself not to bite the fruit and instead thrust it into his jacket pocket. Then he heard the sound of a violin being plucked. Looking up he saw musicians sitting on chairs beneath the nearby trees.

The music began, soft as a whisper spoken by a mother to a sleeping child. Soft and gentle and soothing it was, and Jack Mhor, for all his fears and caution, could not resist the beauty and the sorrow of the melody. He closed his eyes and sank deep into the ever-changing mood of the music as it rose and fell, dipped, curtsied, skipped and paused, reflected, then ran on laughing. As he drifted in the great tonal currents he heard beyond the song of the instruments snatches of older and vaster music; the electric pulsing hiss of planets, the crackle of asteroids spinning in the vast void of the cosmos. Beyond these titan tunes he glimpsed a rose, white and pure and limitless.

He awoke with a gasp, one hand gripping his pain-spiked chest, his vision blurred with tears. Jack Mhor took a deep breath, and wiped the tears from his eyes. He was cold and his clothes damp from the mist-thin rain. It was morning and he was sitting in a field that held no mansion or musicians or magical beings. His only company was a couple of curious cows who looked at him with great brown eyes.

'It was all a dream, my dears,' said Jack Mhor sadly to the two cows. 'A dream and nothing more.' He pushed himself up, and as he did so

something fell from his pocket. There it lay in the mud; a beautiful golden apple. And, oh, what a hunger and a sorrow filled the mud-splattered Jack Mhor. But he shook himself hard and tugged at the hair on his head, then, breaking free of the spell, walked out of the field and found that he was only a few yards away from the church and the graveyard. He gave a nod of thanks to any fairies that might be around and a quick grateful prayer to God for his salvation, then made his way home.

As for the cows, they left the golden apple well alone, and from what I hear it is there still.

Notes from the Author

I was brought up by stories. My extended family were great at spinning yarns: my parents, uncles, aunts, grandmothers and cousins. Everybody had something to say. Some tales were quirky family history, some were more strange accounts of ghosts and curious coincidences and, of course, the devil himself made the occasional appearance.

Some of these stories were told indoors at family gatherings, where the adults all yarned and us little ones listened to it all. But the best stories were told outside. Some of these tales were about the place we were walking through and about how my family fitted into that landscape – who had lived where, done what and when and what strange things had happened to them. All these stories were coloured and shaped by the surrounding landscape, for a story told on a dark woodland path is a lot different to a story told on a beach or on a city street. That love of telling stories is still very alive in my family. My nieces and nephews and my own children can all tell a yarn at the flip of a hat (even our dogs tell stories!).

Books were and are a big part of my life. Long before I could read, I loved books. Both my mother and father took time to read to me and my siblings; the memory of those quieter moments remain with me. My father, licking his finger before turning a page; my mother's warm voice reading *The Owl and the Pussy Cat*. I love books and I love places filled with books. I am the person you see wandering around a bookshop or library with eyes wide with wonder.

My advice, then, for anybody interested in collecting or writing stories is to listen, walk and read. Oh yes, and remember the best creativity apps you can access are your parents, grandparents and guardians. Feel free to ask them about what life was like when they were your age. What was school like? What was their favourite holiday? What about their first visit to the doctor? How did they celebrate the big festivals that mark the year – Easter, Ramadan, Samhain, Diwali, Hanukkah, or Christmas? And, of course, what stories were they told as a child? Where was the story told? Who told it? Who else was there? What food and drink, and scents and sounds surrounded that telling?

And what about the fairies – do any of your elders have stories about them? They may do or they may not, but here is a curious fact: the good people, *na daoine mhaithe*, the immortals – whatever you want to call them – love stories. When you listen to a story it is very possible that a fairy – invisible or in disguise – will be right beside you listening intently …